P9-CRA-683

I HEAR A NOISE

DIANE GOODE

E. P. DUTTON · NEW YORK

NOV 7 '88

Library of Congress Cataloging-in-Publication Data
Goode, Diane.   I hear a noise.

Summary: A little boy, hearing noises at his window
at bedtime, calls for his mother. His worst fears are
realized, but he learns that monsters have mothers too.

[1. Monsters—Fiction.   2. Bedtime—Fiction.
3. Fear—Fiction.   4. Imagination—Fiction]   I. Title.
PZ7.G604Iab   1988   [E]   87-3060
ISBN 0-525-44353-3

Published in the United States by E. P. Dutton,
2 Park Avenue, New York, N.Y. 10016,
a division of NAL Penguin Inc.

Published simultaneously in Canada by
Fitzhenry & Whiteside Limited, Toronto

Editor: Ann Durell   Designer: Riki Levinson

Printed in Hong Kong by South China Printing Co.
First Edition   COBE   10 9 8 7 6 5 4 3 2 1

for Papa

"Mother! I hear a noise!"

"It's only the wind. Now go to sleep.
Good night."

"MOTHER! I hear it again!"

"It's just a branch against the window.
Sleep tight."

"MOTHER!"

"Oh my!"

"We're home!"

"What have you got there?"

"None of your business!"

"MOTHER!"

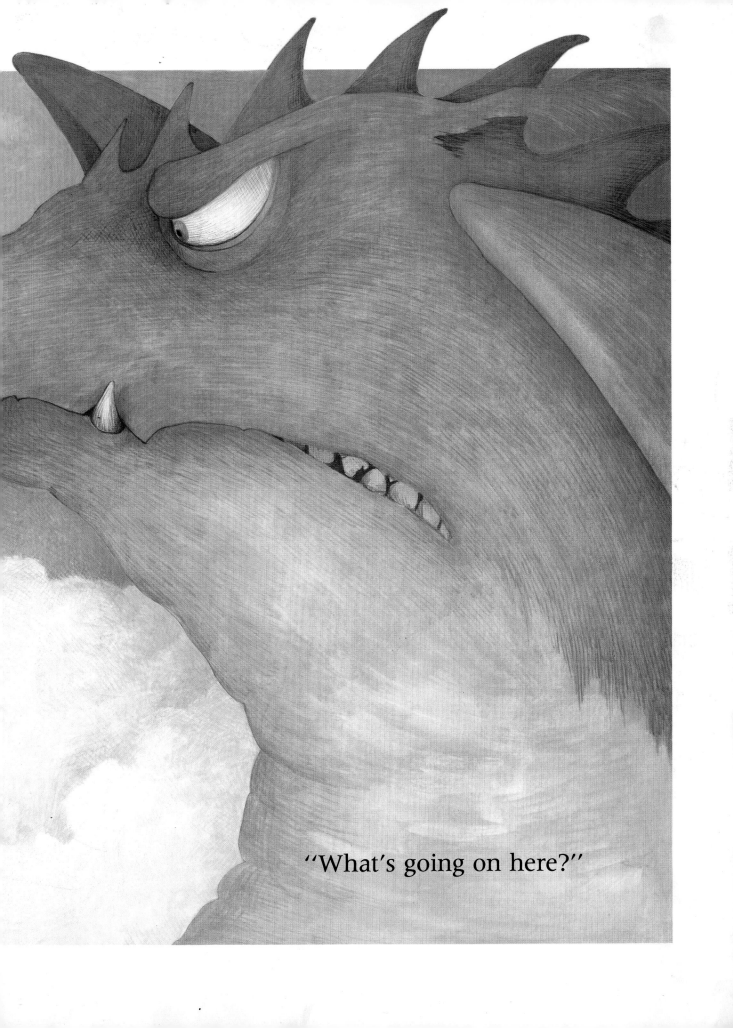

"What's going on here?"

"You should all be ashamed."

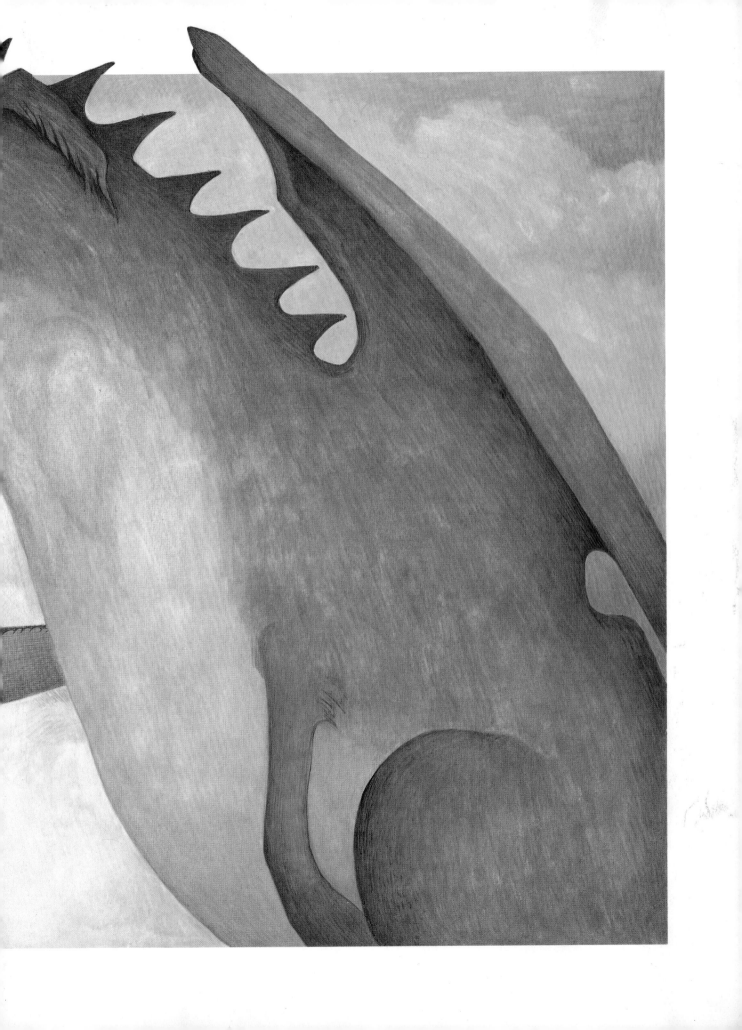

"I want you to take them right
back where you found them . . .
and don't ever touch them again."

"Good night."

"Sleep tight."